The Little Bear Stories

Can't You Sleep, Little Bear?

Let's Go Home, Little Bear

You and Me, Little Bear

Well Done, Little Bear

Martin Waddell
Illustrated by **Barbara Firth**

WALKER BOOKS
AND SUBSIDIARIES
LONDON · BOSTON · SYDNEY

First published individually as
Can't You Sleep, Little Bear? (1988),
Let's Go Home, Little Bear (1991),
You and Me, Little Bear (1996) and
Well Done, Little Bear (1999)
by Walker Books Ltd,
87 Vauxhall Walk, London SE11 5HJ

This edition published 2001

2 4 6 8 10 9 7 5 3 1

Text © 1988, 1991, 1996, 1999 Martin Waddell
Illustrations © 1988, 1999; 1991, 1999; 1996, 1999; 1999 Barbara Firth

The right of Martin Waddell to be identified as author of this work has been
asserted by him in accordance with the Copyright, Designs and Patents Act 1988

This book has been typeset in Columbus

Printed in Hong Kong

British Library Cataloguing in Publication Data:
a catalogue record for this book is available from the British Library

ISBN 0-7445-8154-0

Can't You Sleep, Little Bear?

Once there were two bears,
Big Bear and Little Bear.
Big Bear is the big bear, and Little Bear is the little bear.
They played all day in the bright sunlight. When
night came, and the sun went down, Big Bear took
Little Bear home to the Bear Cave.

Big Bear put Little Bear to bed in the dark
part of the cave. "Go to sleep, Little Bear," he said.

And Little Bear tried.

Big Bear settled in the Bear Chair and
read his Bear Book, by the light of the fire.

But Little Bear couldn't get to sleep.

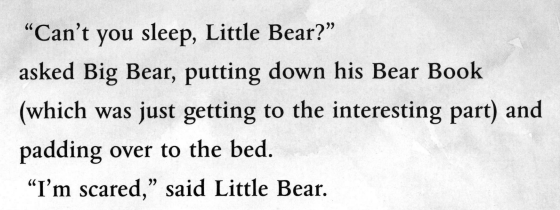

"Can't you sleep, Little Bear?"
asked Big Bear, putting down his Bear Book
(which was just getting to the interesting part) and
padding over to the bed.
 "I'm scared," said Little Bear.
"Why are you scared, Little Bear?" asked Big Bear.
"I don't like the dark," said Little Bear.
"What dark?" said Big Bear.
"The dark all around us,"
said Little Bear.

Big Bear looked, and he saw that the dark part of the cave was very dark, so he went to the Lantern Cupboard and took out the tiniest lantern that was there.

Big Bear lit the tiniest lantern, and put it near to Little Bear's bed.

"There's a tiny light to stop you being scared, Little Bear," said Big Bear.

"Thank you, Big Bear," said Little Bear, cuddling up in the glow.

"Now go to sleep, Little Bear," said Big Bear, and he padded back to the Bear Chair and settled down to read the Bear Book, by the light of the fire.

Little Bear tried to go to sleep, but he couldn't.

"Can't you sleep, Little Bear?" yawned Big Bear, putting down his Bear Book (with just four pages to go to the interesting bit) and padding over to the bed.

"I'm scared," said Little Bear.

"Why are you scared, Little Bear?" asked Big Bear.

"I don't like the dark," said Little Bear.

"What dark?" said Big Bear.

"The dark all around us," said Little Bear.

"But I brought you a lantern!" said Big Bear.

"Only a tiny-weeny one," said Little Bear. "And there's lots of dark!"

Big Bear looked, and he saw that Little Bear was quite right, there was still lots of dark. So Big Bear went to the Lantern Cupboard and took out a bigger lantern.

Big Bear lit the lantern, and put it beside the other one.

"Now go to sleep, Little Bear,"
said Big Bear and he padded back to the Bear Chair
and settled down to read the Bear Book,
by the light of the fire.
Little Bear tried and tried to go to sleep,
but he couldn't.

"Can't you sleep,
Little Bear?"
grunted Big Bear, putting
down his Bear Book
(with just three pages to go)
and padding over to the bed.

"I'm scared," said Little Bear.

"Why are you scared, Little Bear?" asked Big Bear.

"I don't like the dark," said Little Bear.

"What dark?" asked Big Bear.

"The dark all around us," said Little Bear.

"But I brought you two lanterns!" said Big Bear. "A tiny
one and a bigger one!"

"Not much bigger," said Little Bear. "And there's still
lots of dark."

Big Bear thought about it, and then he went
to the Lantern Cupboard and took out
the Biggest Lantern of Them All, with two
handles and a bit of chain. He hooked
the lantern up above Little Bear's bed.
"I've brought you the Biggest Lantern
of Them All!" he told Little Bear. "That's
to stop you being scared!"
"Thank you, Big Bear," said Little Bear,
curling up in the glow and watching
the shadows dance.
"Now go to sleep, Little Bear," said Big Bear
and he padded back to the Bear Chair and
settled down to read the Bear Book,
by the light of the fire.

Little Bear tried and tried and
tried to go to sleep,
but he couldn't.

"Can't you sleep, Little Bear?" groaned Big Bear,
putting down his Bear Book
(with just two pages to go)
    and padding over to the bed.

"I'm scared," said Little Bear.

"Why are you scared, Little Bear?" asked Big Bear.

"I don't like the dark," said Little Bear.

"What dark?" asked Big Bear.

"The dark all around us," said Little Bear.

"But I brought you the Biggest Lantern of Them All, and there isn't any dark left," said Big Bear.

"Yes, there is!" said Little Bear. "There is, out there!"

And he pointed out of the Bear Cave, at the night.

Big Bear saw that Little Bear was right.
Big Bear was very puzzled. All the lanterns in the
world couldn't light up the dark outside.

Big Bear thought about it for a long time, and
then he said, "Come on, Little Bear."

"Where are we going?" asked Little Bear.

"Out!" said Big Bear.

"Out into the darkness?" said Little Bear.

"Yes!" said Big Bear.

"But I'm scared of the dark!" said Little Bear.

"No need to be!" said Big Bear, and he took
Little Bear by the paw and led him out from the
cave into the night

and it was ...

DARK!

"Ooooh! I'm scared," said Little Bear,
cuddling up to Big Bear.
Big Bear lifted Little Bear, and
cuddled him, and said, "Look at the dark,
Little Bear." And Little Bear looked.

"I've brought you the moon, Little Bear," said Big Bear.
"The bright yellow moon, and all the twinkly stars."

But Little Bear didn't say anything, for he had gone
to sleep, warm and safe in Big Bear's arms.

Big Bear carried Little Bear back into the Bear Cave,
fast asleep, and he settled down with Little Bear
on one arm and the Bear Book on the other, cosy
in the Bear Chair by the fire.

And Big Bear read the Bear Book right to ...

Let's Go Home, Little Bear

Once there were two bears,
Big Bear and Little Bear.
Big Bear is the big bear
and Little Bear is the little bear.
They went for a walk in the woods.

They walked and they walked and
they walked until Big Bear said,
"Let's go home, Little Bear."
So they started back home on the
path through the woods.

PLOD PLOD PLOD
went Big Bear, plodding along.
Little Bear ran on in front,
jumping and sliding
and having great fun.

And then...
Little Bear stopped
and he listened
and then he turned round
and he looked.

"Come on, Little Bear," said Big Bear,
but Little Bear didn't stir.

"I thought I heard something!" Little Bear said.

"What did you hear?" said Big Bear.

"Plod, plod, plod," said Little Bear.
"I think it's a Plodder!"

Big Bear turned round and
he listened and looked.

No Plodder was there.

"Let's go home, Little Bear," said Big Bear.
"The plod was my feet in the snow."

They set off again on the path
through the woods.
   PLOD PLOD PLOD
went Big Bear with Little Bear
walking beside him,
just glancing a bit, now and again.

   And then...
Little Bear stopped
and he listened
and then he turned round
and he looked.

"Come on, Little Bear," said Big Bear,
but Little Bear didn't stir.
   "I thought I heard something!"
Little Bear said.
   "What did you hear?" said Big Bear.
   "Drip, drip, drip," said Little Bear.
"I think it's a Dripper!"

Big Bear turned round,
and he listened and looked.
No Dripper was there.
"Let's go home, Little Bear,"
said Big Bear.
"That was the ice as it dripped
in the stream."

They set off again on the
path through the woods.
    PLOD PLOD PLOD
went Big Bear with Little Bear
closer beside him.

    And then...
Little Bear stopped
and he listened
and then he turned round
and he looked.

"Come on, Little Bear," said Big Bear,
but Little Bear didn't stir.

"I know I heard something this time!"
Little Bear said.

"What did you hear?" said Big Bear.

"Plop, plop, plop," said Little Bear.
"I think it's a Plopper."

Big Bear turned round,
and he listened and looked.
No Plopper was there.
"Let's go home, Little Bear,"
said Big Bear.
"That was the snow plopping
down from a branch."

PLOD PLOD PLOD
went Big Bear along the path
through the woods.
But Little Bear walked
slower and slower
and at last he sat
down in the snow.

"Come on, Little Bear," said Big Bear.
"It is time we were both back home."
But Little Bear sat and said nothing.
"Come on and be carried,"
said Big Bear.

Big Bear put Little Bear
high up on his back,
and set off down the path
through the woods.

WOO WOO WOO
"It is only the wind, Little Bear,"
said Big Bear and he walked
on down the path.

CREAK CREAK CREAK
"It is only the trees, Little Bear,"
said Big Bear and he walked
on down the path.

PLOD PLOD PLOD
"It is only the sound of my feet
again," said Big Bear and he
plodded on and on and on
until they came back home
to their cave.

Big Bear and Little Bear
went down into the dark,
the dark of their own
Bear Cave.

"Just stay there, Little Bear,"
said Big Bear, putting
Little Bear in the Bear Chair
with a blanket to keep him warm.
   Big Bear stirred up the fire from
the embers and lighted the lamps
and made the Bear Cave
all cosy again.
   "Now tell me a story,"
Little Bear said.

And Big Bear sat down in the Bear Chair
with Little Bear curled on his lap.
And he told a story of Plodders
and Drippers and Ploppers
and the sounds of the snow
in the woods,
and this Little Bear
and this Big Bear
plodding all the way ...

HOME

You and Me, Little Bear

Once there were two bears,
Big Bear and Little Bear.
Big Bear is the big bear
and Little Bear is the little bear.
Little Bear wanted to play, but
Big Bear had things to do.

"I want to play!" Little Bear said.
"I've got to get wood for the fire,"
said Big Bear.

"I'll get some too," Little Bear said.
"You and me, Little Bear," said Big Bear.
"We'll fetch the wood in together!"

"What shall we do now?" Little Bear asked.

"I'm going for water," said Big Bear.

"Can I come too?" Little Bear asked.

"You and me, Little Bear," said Big Bear.

"We'll go for the water together."

"Now we can play," Little Bear said.

"I've still got to tidy our cave," said Big Bear.

"Well ... I'll tidy too!" Little Bear said.

"You and me," said Big Bear.

"You tidy your things, Little Bear.

I'll look after the rest."

"I've tidied my things, Big Bear!"
Little Bear said.

"That's good, Little Bear," said Big Bear.
"But I'm not finished yet."

"I want you to play!" Little Bear said.

"You'll have to play by yourself,
Little Bear," said Big Bear.
"I've still got plenty to do!"

Little Bear went to play by
himself, while Big Bear
got on with the work.

Little Bear played
bear-jump.

Little Bear

played

bear-slide.

Little Bear played
bear-swing.

Little Bear played
bear-tricks-with-bear-sticks.

Little Bear played bear-stand-on-his-head
and Big Bear came out to sit on his rock.

Little Bear played bear-run-about-by-himself
and Big Bear closed his
eyes for a think.

Little Bear went to
speak to Big Bear,
but Big Bear was ...

asleep!

"Wake up, Big Bear!" Little Bear said.
Big Bear opened his eyes.
"I've played all my games
by myself," Little Bear said.

Big Bear thought for a bit, then he said,
"Let's play hide-and-seek, Little Bear."
"I'll hide and you seek," Little Bear said,
and he ran off to hide.

"I'm coming now!" Big Bear called,
and he looked till he
found Little Bear.

Then Big Bear hid, and Little Bear looked.
"I found you, Big Bear!" Little Bear said.
"Now I'll hide again."

They played lots of bear-games.
When the sun slipped away through
the trees, they were still playing.
Then Little Bear said,
"Let's go home now, Big Bear."

Big Bear and Little Bear went
home to their cave.
"We've been busy today, Little Bear!"
said Big Bear.
"It was lovely, Big Bear," Little Bear
said. "Just you and me playing ...

together."

Well Done, Little Bear

Once there were two bears,
Big Bear and Little Bear.
Big Bear is the big bear
and Little Bear is the little bear.
One day, Little Bear wanted
to go exploring.
Little Bear led the way.

Little Bear found Bear Rock.
"Look at me!" Little Bear said.
"Where are you, Little Bear?" asked Big Bear.
"I'm exploring Bear Rock,"
Little Bear said. "Watch me climb."
"Well done, Little Bear,"
said Big Bear.

"I need you now, Big Bear,"
Little Bear shouted. "I'm jumping."
"I'm here, Little Bear," said Big Bear.
Little Bear jumped off Bear Rock
into the arms of Big Bear.
"I'm off exploring again!"
Little Bear said and he ran
on in front of Big Bear.

Little Bear found
the old bendy tree.
"Look at me!" Little Bear said.
"I'm bouncing about
on the old bendy tree!"

Little Bear bounced on the branch.
"Watch me bounce higher,
Big Bear!" Little Bear said.
"Well done, Little Bear," said Big Bear.

"Are you ready, Big Bear?"
Little Bear called to Big Bear.

Little Bear bounced
higher and higher

and he bounced
off the branch ...

right into the arms of Big Bear.

"You caught me again!" Little Bear said.

"Well done, Little Bear," said Big Bear.

"I'm going exploring some more!"
Little Bear said.

Little Bear found the stream, just by the dark bit.
"I'm going over the stream," Little Bear said.
"Look at me, Big Bear. Look at me crossing
the stream by myself."
"Well done, Little Bear,"
said Big Bear.

Little Bear hopped from one stone to another.
"I'm the best hopper there is!" Little Bear said.
Little Bear hopped again,
and again.

"Take care, Little Bear," said Big Bear.

"I am taking care," Little Bear said.

"Little Bear...!"

called Big Bear...

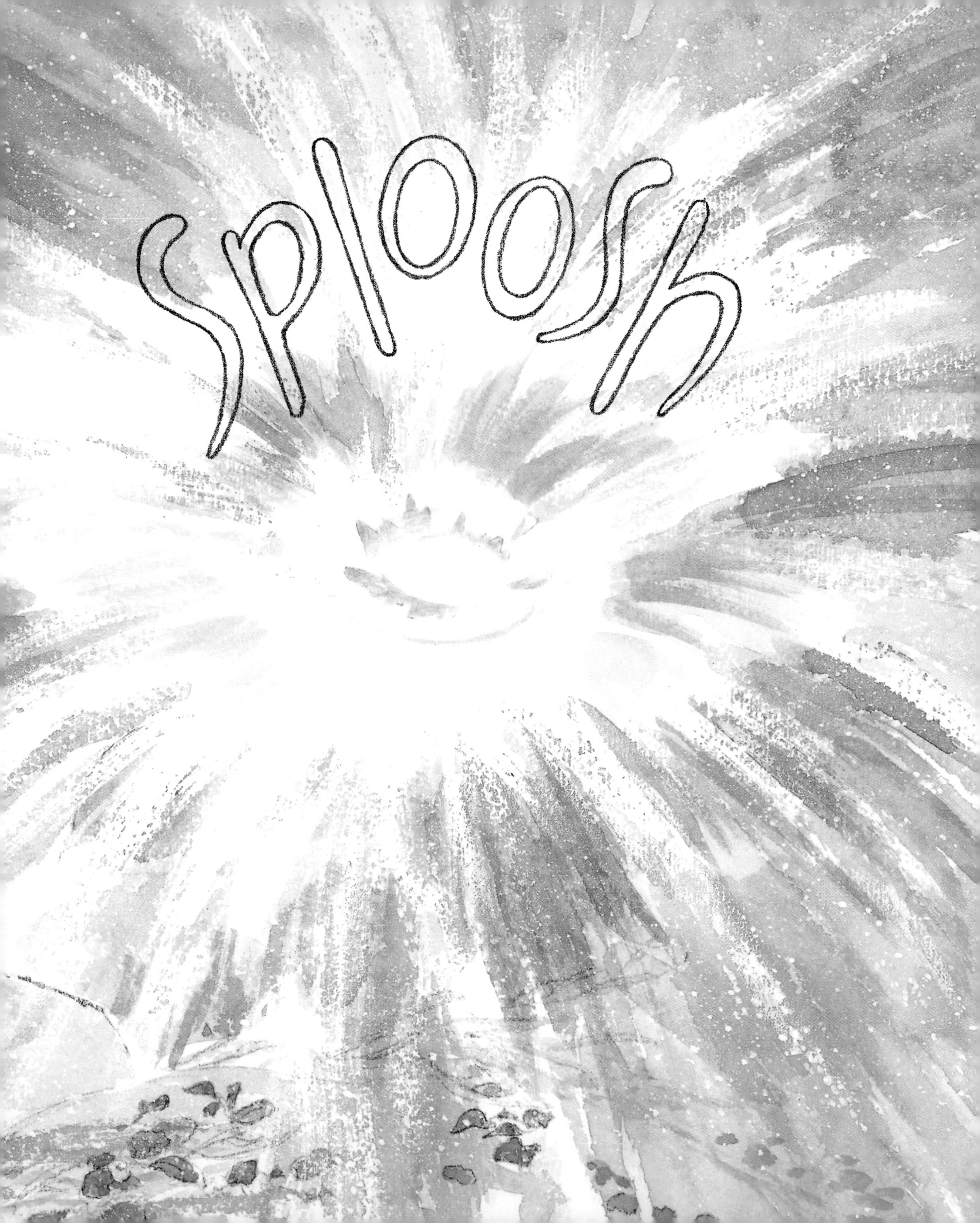
sploosh

"Help me, Big Bear,"
Little Bear cried.

Big Bear waded in, and he pulled
Little Bear out of the water.
"Don't cry, Little Bear," Big Bear said.
"We'll soon have you dry."
He hugged Little Bear.

"Let's go exploring some more,
Little Bear," said Big Bear.

"Exploring where?" Little Bear asked.

"On the far side of the stream," said Big Bear.

"Take care, Big Bear, you might fall
in like me," Little Bear said.

"Not if you show me the stone
where you slipped," said Big Bear.

"It was this stone," Little Bear said.

"Well done, Little Bear!"
said Big Bear.

Big Bear and Little Bear explored
their way home through the woods,
all the way back to the Bear Cave.

Big Bear and Little Bear settled down
cosy and warm in the Bear Chair.

"Were you scared, Little Bear?" asked Big Bear.
"Were you scared when you fell in the water?"

"I knew you'd be there," Little Bear said.

"That's right, Little Bear," said Big Bear.

"I'll be there when
you need me ...

always."